THE CRUISE OF THE
BREADWINNER

PIP
POLLINGER IN PRINT

Pollinger Limited
9 Staple Inn
Holborn
LONDON
WC1V 7QH

www.pollingerltd.com

First published in Great Britain in 1946 by Michael Joseph
This large print edition published by Pollinger in Print 2007

A CIP catalogue record is available from the British Library

ISBN 978-1-905665-37-2

THE CRUISE OF THE BREADWINNER

H. E. Bates

FIRST PUBLISHED 1946

AS SHE WENT DOWN THE ESTUARY ON THE YELLOW tide between wintry stretches of salt-white marshland, *The Breadwinner* had the look of a discarded and battered toy. She was one of those small lugsail fishing boats that in peace-time lie up the mud reaches of southern rivers, going out on one tide and back on the next, indistinguishable from hundreds of her kind. Her deck-house, not much larger than a dog-kennel and once painted butchers' blue, was now daubed with broad veins of war-grey put on with a whitewash brush, and her sail had been furled untidily to the mast like a copper umbrella. On all her grey fabric they were the only touches of colour except the white lettering of her name. Aft she carried a Lewis gun that had never been fired in the twenty years between the wars, and that had now something of the appearance of a patent frying-pan. She looked very old and very slow. Yet in ten minutes she had cleared the estuary and the long sandy point beyond and was well to seaward, heading due east up the Channel, rolling slightly on the light westward cross-wind of the early day.

Gregson stood at the wheel in the thirty-eight inches of space that separated it from the hatchway. He could just squeeze himself in. The curve of his belly caught the spokes of the wheel where they met the hub. In the course of months this friction would rub a neat oblong hole in the three layers of his jerseys, going finally down to the seam of his shirt. When this happened Gregson would turn the three jerseys round and wear them back to front. He had once been a man of six feet three, but now he had the slight downward curve of a man who is constantly about to stoop to pick something up but sees only the eighteen-stone mass of his own flesh hiding whatever it was he was trying to find below. Sometimes when he held the wheel in one hand and turned his massive grey head first skyward, to look at the weather, and then downward, to bawl at the crew of two below, he was so enormous and he held the wheel so casually that it might have been a watch.

All day he bawled blasting conversation into the hatch below.

"Gittin' that tea ready, Snowy?"

"Yeh!" The boy's voice from below was drawled out, and sometimes, when surprised, squeaky because it had not fully broken.

"Well then, git it ready!"

"Yeh!"

"Yeh what? What did I tell you?"

"I dunno."

"You dunno eh? Well, I'll bleedin' make you know. Ain't I allus told you call the skipper mister? Ain't that what I told ye'? Ain't it?"

"Yeh."

"Yeh what?"

"Yeh, mister——"

"It don't matter now! Too late! Git that tea!"

If there was ever a smile on the face of Gregson as he yelled all this, the boy, down below, warming the enamel teapot on the stove of a galley three feet by four, never saw it. It appeared to him always as if Gregson were a man of unappeasable frenzy.

"How's that injun going, Jimmy?"

Gregson never succeeded in getting an answer to that question first time. It was Jimmy's excuse that the noise of the

7

eighteen-horse auxiliary drowned even what Gregson could say.

"Jimmy!"

"Hullo."

Jimmy came and stood at the foot of the gangway, dark and pessimistic, looking up, mouth awry, as if the left side of his face were paralytic with pain. He was a man given to violent depressions and upliftings of temper for no reason at all. "Hullo?" he said again. The word had in it the slow challenge of a man full of all sorts of unknown and incalculable trouble. It was partly inspired by habitual dislike of everything aboard and about and belonging to *The Breadwinner*. It was partly the voice of a man weary of the nuisances of a lousy small boat that should have been on the scrap-heap, with a rotten engine in need of a re-bore that was for ever breaking down. It was an exceedingly long-suffering voice, and the fact that Gregson never noticed it, or seemed to ignore it if he did, made it more long-suffering still. But it was also partly the voice of a man whose larger pleasure in life is the pleasure of grievance. It was inversely happy among the miseries of *The Breadwinner*. At home Jimmy had a wife and three small children, and it was he who would fire the Lewis gun if ever it were fired.

"I said how's that injun?"

"I told you last time. And the time afore that. And the time afore that."

"Don't tell me it ain't no good, because I know different."

"It ain't so much it ain't no good. What I keep tellin' on yer is we oughta git two engines. Not one. We oughta git two fourteen-horse engines, instead of one eighteen-horse, so's if one goes, we got a spare."

"And supposin' both go?"

"It ain't likely."

"No, it ain't likely. And it ain't likely I'll git the money either. Where's the money coming from?"

"Git the Government to pay it! They got plenty. They throw it about enough, don't they? Git them to pay it. We're on government work, ain't we?"

There were times when Gregson pushed his belly tight against the wheel and held it savagely there and did not answer, and he did it most often when Jimmy talked about the Government. Gregson did not care for the Government. The Government was some huge, anonymous, thwarting, stingy, stinking body empowered to frustrate the lives of ordinary men. Gregson felt for it a more positive enmity than he felt for any living person, enemy or friend. "Don't talk about no bloody government to me."

"Well, don't say I ain't told yer. One o' these fine days we'll get out there, forty miles from nowhere, and she'll go dead on you. And then what?"

"And then what?" Gregson roared. "What the bleedin' hell d'ye think wind and sail is for?"

Gregson stuck his belly harder than ever against the wheel, holding on with both hands, and was silent, looking at the day. Behind him he could see now the coast of England becoming slowly more coloured in the blue-orange light of morning, with low clean stretches of deserted sand marked as far as he could see with what looked like the rusty stitchery of steel defences, and farther east the sun rising dark red over the terraced and almost all empty white and crimson houses that lay under the line of hills. It was from these hills, becoming still further eastward cliffs that came down to the sea like the carved edges of creamy glaciers, that Gregson saw the first patrol of the day.

"Snowy!"

"Yeh?"

"Planes!"

The boy Snowy came bouncing on deck like a blonde and excited rabbit surprised out of a hole, carrying a teacup in one hand and blinking friendly blue eyes against the strong sea-light. He looked no more than seventeen, his white-yellow hair blown forward by the wind in one thick swathe over his face as he turned to gaze at the land.

"Bunch o' Spits, ain't they, Snowy?" Gregson said.

"Hurricanes."

Gregson did not speak. The boy knew everything; there was no arguing with the boy. Gregson believed that if an entirely new and undocumented plane had come out of the Arctic the boy would have given it a name. The boy knew everything that flew, and a lot, Gregson thought, that had not yet begun to fly. He named them while they were still gnats on the horizon. He could name them at twenty thousand feet, and sometimes by mere sound, not seeing them at all. Without him Gregson would have been utterly lost; *The Breadwinner* could never have done a single patrol.

"Looks like a nice day, anyway," Gregson said, as if that at least were something he could understand.

The boy stood watching the squadron of Hurricanes resolve itself out of the east. It came straight over the cliffs, in two flights line astern, with straight and fine precision, quite slow, wings shining in the sun, as if each aircraft were tied by an invisible string to the other, and then turned westward to follow the line of shore. The noise of engines was never loud enough to drown the noise of *The Breadwinner's* single auxiliary, but it was loud and beautiful enough to bring the engineer-gunner on deck.

"Hurricanes," Gregson said, before the boy could open his mouth.

"Steady, steady. They might be Spits," Jimmy said.

"Ah, Spits your old woman," Gregson said. "Use your eyes."

"One missing," the boy said. "Man short."

"Hell, that they is too," Gregson said. "I never twigged it. Snowy ain't half got a pair, of eyes, ain't he?"

"Just as well," Jimmy said.

Gregson turned to look hard at the engineer, but Jimmy had even in that moment disappeared down the hatchway. On deck the boy followed the course of the Hurricanes over against the thin line of shore with eyes that were lightly fixed in a dream. He was lost in the wonder of contemplation, even when Gregson spoke again.

"Tea ready yit?"

"Just made," the boy said.

"Ah, that's me old beauty. That's a boy. Bring us a cup up, Snowy. I got a throat like a star-fish."

The boy was already going below.

"And you better stop on deck then and do your look-out. Looks like a flying day, don't it?"

The boy said yes, it was a flying day all right, and went down into the galley below and then came back, after a moment or two, with the tea. The cup was a double-size moustache cup that Gregson took and held in one hand like an egg. He began to drink where he stood, plunging his face into the cup and then holding cup and face pressed close together with the palm of his hand. As Gregson drank the boy went forward and stood in the place where he stood on every patrol, in the bows, leaning forward and slightly over the boat's side, like a light figurehead. He went there every morning irritated by the slightest recurrent grievance against Gregson. Long ago, soon after the war had begun, when he had first become boy on *The Breadwinner*, Gregson had promised him a pair of binoculars. Once a week, ever since, the boy had asked Gregson about the glasses, but there was never any sign of them. It appeared to the boy as if Gregson forgot all about them, not deliberately but sometimes out of sheer ineptitude. And then sometimes it seemed as if he forgot them purely by reason of belonging to the larger, more preoccupied, more adult world. Then some-times he found himself slightly afraid of Gregson; but it was a fear purely of size, of the enormity and noisiness of Gregson's flesh. It never matched the enormity of his disappointment at Gregson's constantly unfulfilled promise about the binoculars. To have had the binoculars would have been the most exciting thing on earth: a greater thing than the sea-rescue of a pilot, the wreck of a plane, or even the firing of the Lewis gun. He had longed for all these things to happen on all the patrols of *The Breadwinner* with a bright and narrow desire that kept him awake at night and brought him down to the jetty in the mornings running and with bits of his breakfast still in his hands. But the realization of them would have been nothing beside the sight of Gregson coming down the street between the black fish warehouses carrying a brown leather case over his oilskins.

As he took up his place in the bows he could feel the wind light and smooth on his face as it came out of the west. It had in it that curious winter sea-warmth that was like human breath. It barely broke the face of the sea, which had across it everywhere to the east long quivering drifts of leaf-broken silver light. The sky was smooth too, without any but slightest golden cloud about the sun, the air so clear that he could begin to see the white relief of Northern France before the coast of England had begun to fade, with its dark bird patrol of Hurricanes, behind him.

He leaned on the bows and took in the whole of the smooth winter sea and sky for miles and miles about him, and noted it, more or less unconsciously, as empty. It was empty of sound too. For some time he had been practising spotting by ear, so that now he could tell a Dornier, if ever one came, from a Heinkel, or a Spit from a Hurricane, even though he never saw them. Sometimes it was hard to disentangle these sounds from the sounds of wind and water and give them a name, but on a calm day or even a calm night it was easy, and he was becoming sure and proud of these distinctions.

The Breadwinner had been cruising for a little more than an hour when he suddenly heard firing far across from the south-west. It split the very calm air for about a second, startling first himself and then Gregson into shouting.

"Machine-gunning!" Gregson yelled.

"Yeh! May be testing his guns," the boy said.

"Too far out, ain't it?"

"Listen again!" the boy called.

They listened again, and then as Jimmy came up the hatchway to listen too, carrying his cup of tea in his hands, the burst came over the sea again. It came in a muffled and violent rattle, slightly longer this time. It seemed to come from beyond mid-Channel, a long way from shore.

"That ain't no gun-testing," Gregson said. "Somebody's having a go."

The boy stood intently listening, both hands clasping the boat side, his yellow head far forward, in a sort of contemplated dive.

"I can hear something out there!" the boy said.

"So can we. It ain't sea-gulls either."

"I mean there's a plane out there. Two planes."

"Go on," Jimmy said. "Three planes."

"Ah, shut up," Gregson said. "You allus got your ears bunged up with injun oil."

"I tell y' it's gun-testing," Jimmy said. "They were at it yesterday."

The boy had taken up an attitude of fierce excitement, balanced on the extreme forward edge of the bows, shading his face with his hands.

"There's only two planes," he said. "If Jimmy could shut the engine off I could hear what they were!"

"Go on, Jim," Gregson said, "shut her off."

"Shut off? You want some trouble, don't you?"

"All right, all right, put her in neutral and keep her running."

In the half-silence that came a minute later, with *The Breadwinner* stopped and the engine turning over only with coughs of low and regular vibration, the boy yelled frantically that he heard a Messerschmitt.

"Yeh! but can you see it?" Gregson said.

"No! I can hear it, I can hear it! I tell you I can hear it!" he said.

"What was the other?"

"I dunno. They both gone now. I can't see." It occurred to him suddenly that this was the moment in which he could throw at Gregson the subject of the binoculars, but his excitement soared up inside him in a flame that burnt out and obliterated in a moment all other thought. "We ought to have a look!" he shouted.

Gregson became excited too. "All right, why don't we?" The rolls of flesh on his throat were suddenly tautened in an amazing way as he lifted his head and strained to look westward, bawling at the same time, "What in bleedin' hell are we supposed to be for?"

"There's more firing!" the boy shouted.

"I'm turning her round, Jimmy," Gregson said, "as soon as you can git her away."

"Waste o' bloody time, I tell y' it's practice firing," Jimmy said, and went below.

The boy, jumping back on deck and turning to see the gigantic face of Gregson still so tautly uplifted that it was like the face of a great bronze-red sea-lion straining to catch something, felt in that moment the beginnings of a new emotion about Gregson. He felt that he loved him. And he felt also that he came very near to despising the engineer.

GREGSON CRUISED *THE BREADWINNER* AT THREE-quarter speed for about half an hour in a direction roughly opposite to the path of light made by the sun on the sea. It was Gregson's impression as they went farther west that a haze was gathering low down against the horizon but far beyond the possible limit of patrol. It was nowhere thick enough to have any colour or any effect on the light of the sea. All the time the boy stood in the bows of the boat, shading his eyes. He had a sort of fierce and transfixed uneasiness about him. Jimmy had come on deck.

"I don't see much," he said. "I don't hear much either."

They were far enough westward now to be out of sight of land.

"You want so much for your bleedin' money," Gregson said, and left his mouth open to emit a belch like a wet explosion. "Ah, belch-guts," he said. "Tea coming up," and heaved his belly forward to give a second belch that was like a wetter, deeper echo of the first.

"What's ahead, Snowy boy?"

"Keep quiet! Keep quiet!" the boy said.

"No wonder the kid can't hear," Jimmy said, and actually smiled.

"What is it?" Gregson roared.

"Can Jimmy shut off?" the boy said.

"No wonder he can't," Gregson said. "What d'ye want shut off for?" he yelled.

"I can hear something—a whistle or something—something like a whistle——"

"A whistle be God!" Gregson said. "Shut her off, Jimmy! A whistle!"

In the interval of Jimmy going below and the engine being shut off in a series of choked bursts of the exhaust, *The Breadwinner* travelled about a quarter of a mile. It was far enough to bring within the boy's vision a new space of sea and within his hearing the faint but madly repeated note of the whistle he had already heard. He stood waving his arms as Gregson came blundering forward up the narrow deck like a groping and excited bullock. "Hey, what is it, Snowy, what is it? What ye twigged, Snowy boy?" His wind came belching up with his words in a wet gollop for which he was this time too surprised to have any comment.

"Can you hear it?" the boy said. "Can you hear it? The whistle!"

They listened together, Gregson leaning forward across the bows of the boat, his face almost instantly lit up. "Be God, Snowy, that ain't fur off!" he said. "It ain't fur off, Snowy!"

By now the boy was not listening. He was mutely arrested by the conviction that far across to westward he could see something that might have been a floating cockle-shell. It had sometimes the appearance of a ring of transfixed sunlight, caught just below the short horizon visible from a boat that was herself only a few feet above the sea. He held his silence a little longer to himself before he was quite sure. Then he began shouting: "It's a dinghy!" he shouted. "It's a dinghy! I can see it. I can see it! A dinghy!"

"Wheer?" Gregson said. "Wheer, Snowy boy?" He made a sort of mock effort to fling one leg over the side of the boat, and instead lurched fatly forward, breathing heavily under the pressure of his colossal belly.

"Full ahead!" the boy said. "Full ahead!"

He heard his words go aft like a bellowed echo, so loud that in about twenty seconds an answer came in the noise of the engine. Gregson marvelled acidly. "We got going fust bang! Don't say nothing, Snowy. Don't bleedin' well breathe, boy. We got going fust bang!"

Two minutes later the boy was shouting: "Now can you see it? Now, Mister Gregson, if you can't see it now you're as—— Oh! if we had the binoculars we would have seen it sooner."

Gregson, seeing the yellow rubber dinghy at the moment, made no comment on the binoculars, and the subject even for the boy was instantly blown away by gusts of fresh excitement. He could see the man in the dinghy quite clearly now, and from that moment onward began to see him more and more sharply defined in the sunlight until even Gregson, straining forward over the bows more than ever like a raw-necked seal, could see him too. The sight broke on Gregson with the effect of sublime discovery. "I see the bloke!" he roared. "I see the bloke, Snowy. Clear as bleedin' hell! I can see his head plain!"

"He's wearing his flying jacket," the boy said. "And a red muffler with white spots."

To that Gregson had nothing to say, and three or four minutes later they came up with the dinghy and the figure which for the boy had long been so clearly defined. Gregson lumbered aft to yell down to Jimmy the order to stop, and then lumbered forward again in time to see the dinghy drifting close alongside. The young man in the dinghy had never stopped blowing his whistle. He was blowing it now, only taking it from his mouth at last to wave it at Gregson and the boy with a sort of mocking salutation.

"Bloody good whistle!"

"All right?" Gregson yelled over the side. "Ain't hurt or nothing?"

"Right as a pip. Wizard."

"Glad we seed you," Gregson said. "A coupla feet closer, and we'll git y' in."

"Bloody good show," the young man said.

As the dinghy came nearer, finally bumping softly against the boatside, the boy remained motionless, held in speechless fascination by the figure in the flying jacket. It grinned up at him with a sublime youthfulness that to the boy seemed heroically mature. The young man had a mass of thick light-brown hair that curled in heavy waves, and a light, almost corn-brown moustache that flowed stiffly outward until it was dead level with the boundaries of his face. He seemed to have decided to check it there. It gave to his entire appearance and to whatever he did and said an air of light fancy. It proclaimed him as serious about nothing; not even about wars or dinghies or the menace of the sea; least of all about himself.

Gregson and the boy helped to pull him on deck. The boy, looking down, brought to the large muffling flying-boots a little more of the wonder he had brought to the face.

"Sure you're all right? Cold?" Gregson said. "Cuppa tea?"

"Thanks," the youth said. "I'm fine."

Jimmy came up from below and walked forward: so that suddenly the small narrow deck of *The Breadwinner* seemed to become vastly overcrowded.

"Sort o' thing you don't wanna do too often," Gregson said: "ain't it?"

"Third time," the young man said. "Getting used to it now."

"Spit pilot?"

"Typhoon," the pilot said.

"There y'are, Snowy. Typhoons. What was you gittin' up to?" he said to the young man. "Summat go wrong?"

"One of those low-level sods," the young man said. "Chased him all across the Marshes at nought feet. Gave him two squirts and then he started playing tricks. Glycol and muck, pouring out everywhere. Never had a bloody clue and yet kept on, right down on the deck, bouncing up and down, foxing like hell. He must have known he'd had it." The young man paused to look round at the sea. "He was a brave sod. The bravest sod I ever saw."

"Don't you believe it," Gregson said. "Coming in and machine-gunning kids at low-level. That ain't brave."

"This was brave," the young man said.

He spoke with the tempered air of the man who has seen the battle, his words transcending for the first time the comedy of the moustache. He carried suddenly an air of cautious defined authority, using words that there was no contesting.

Gregson, pondering incredibly on this remark about the bravery of enemies, said: "What happened to you then after that?"

"Pranged," the pilot said. "Couldn't pull out. Hit it with a bang."

"And what happened to him?"

The young man looked steadily over the sea, on which the yellow winter sunlight now lay with a sort of hazy unripeness, dissolving itself tenderly towards the almost colourless edges of sky.

"That's what I want to find out," he said.

"You better have a cuppa tea," Gregson said. "Never mind about Jerry. If he's in the sea we'll find him plenty soon enough. He'll wash up."

"I'd like to see what he's like," the boy said. "God, he was brave."

"You think you hit him?" Gregson said.

"I know I hit him."

"Then that's bleedin' good enough, ain't it?" Gregson looked round, heaving his belly, with an air of heavy finality. "Snowy, git us all another cuppa tea!"

The boy turned and went instantly down the hatchway, sliding the last four steps on the smooth heels of his sea-boots. The largeness of the world of men on deck seemed now to narrow down and diminish the already awkward spaces of the tiny cabin below. It oppressed him terribly. He lumbered about it as if he were as large as Gregson, partly stupefied with excitement, partly trying to listen through the cabin-roof to whatever might be going on above. He found an extra cup in the cupboard under the bunks and put it on the table with the two others. He saw it was slightly dirty, and wiped it with his sweater. Then he filled the cups with tea that was in colour something like dark beer. The teapot held about three pints of it, and he filled it up from the big tin kettle before putting it back on the stove. Then he spooned quantities of soft sugar into the cups and stirred each of them madly before taking it upstairs. The whole business took him about three minutes, and he did not think that in this time anything of great importance could have happened on deck.

He was astonished, coming up into the sunlight with the three cups of tea skilfully hooked by their handles into the crook of his first fingers, that even in those few moments a change had taken place. He came up in time to hear Jimmy saying:

"I never knowed it was part of the game to go cruisin' round picking Jerries up."

"I don't know that he's there to pick up," the pilot said. "The bastard is probably dead. All I'm saying is he was a brave bastard."

"That suits me," Gregson said. "If he's dead he's dead. If he ain't he ain't. Have it which way you like, it's all I care."

The boy came with the tea and stood silent, fascinated, while each of the three men took their cups from him. He watched the young pilot, holding his tea in both hands, the fur collar of his flying jacket turned up so that the scarlet muffler on his neck was concealed, look away southward over the sea. It was very like a picture of a pilot he had once cut out of a Sunday paper. To see it in reality at last held him motionlessly bound in a new dream.

"How far do you cruise out?" the young man said.

Gregson had a superstitious horror of cruising down Channel to the west. Fifty years of consistent routine had taken him eastward, fishing in unadventurous waters somewhere between South Foreland and Ostend. He did not like the west for any reason he could say; he did not, for that matter, like the south either. There lurked within him somewhere the cumbrous superstition born of habit, never defined enough to be given a name.

"Well, we're out now about as far as we reckon to go. Don't you wanna git back?"

The pilot, not answering, seemed to measure the caution of Gregson as he gazed across the water. And it occurred suddenly to the boy, watching his face, that he knew perfectly that there were no limits to which Gregson, in human need, would not go. But eastward or westward it was the same as far as enemy pilots were concerned.

And then suddenly the boy remembered something. He spoke to the pilot for the first time.

"How far out did you fire?" he said.

"Smack over a Martello tower," the pilot said, "on the shore."

"Then it wasn't you firing," the boy said. "What we heard was right out to sea."

"Be God so it were," Gregson said. "So it were."

"Mean there was someone else having a go?" the pilot said.

"Sounded like gun-testing," Jimmy said.

"Don't take no bleedin' notice of him," Gregson said. "Was they any more of your blokes out?"

"A whole flight was up."

"There y'are then!" Gregson said. "What are we farting about here for? Warm her up, Jimmy. Let's git on!"

As *The Breadwinner* swung round, turning a point or two south-eastward, sharp into the sun, the boy went forward into the bows and discovered a second or two later that the pilot was there beside him, still warming his fingers on the tea-cup and sometimes reflectively drinking from it, balancing the two wings of the ridiculous corn-ginger moustache on its edges. It did not occur to the boy that he did not look like a fighting man; it occurred to him instead that he might be a man with binoculars. "If we had a pair o' glasses we might pick things up easier," he said.

"Never carry any," the pilot said.

If there was any disappointment in the boy's face it was lost in the ardent gleam of steady and serious wonder which he now brought to bear on the sea. Gradually the sunlight everywhere was losing its lemon pallor, but it was still low enough to lay across the water the long leaf-broken path of difficult and dazzling light. The boy shaded his eyes against it with both hands. He desired to do something remotely professional; something to impress the man of battles standing beside him. He longed dramatically to spot something in the sea. They stood there together for about five minutes, not speaking but both watching with hands framing their-faces against the dazzle of sea-light, and nothing happening or moving except *The Breadwinner* lugging slowly south-eastward out of sight of either shore, the sea emptier and more peaceful than on a peace-time day, until suddenly far behind them Gregson called the boy:

"I'm gittin' peckish, Snowy boy. Ain't peeled them taters yit, ayah?"

"No, mister," the boy said.

"Well, you better git in and peel 'em then. Peel a double dose. Pilots eat same as we do."

The boy said, looking up at the pilot: "I gotta git below now. I'll take your cup down if you've finished." Hating to go, he came also within a short distance of hating Gregson. The pilot finished the tea. "Want another cup? I can bring it," the boy said. "Easy bring it."

"No," the pilot said. "That was fine."

The boy went below, stumbling about the gangway and the cabin as if partially blinded by sun. The remoteness of the world above him was exaggerated by the sound of Jimmy going up the hatchway, leaving him alone with the fire in the toy galley, a sack of potatoes and a jack-knife. He glanced about the box of a cabin, hating it without really seeing its dingy and confined outlines. He thought dismally that nothing ever went on below, that nothing could ever happen there. He longed passionately to talk to the pilot, up in the sun.

Sometimes as he sat there peeling potatoes at the cabin-table he could hear the voice of Gregson from up above, always huge and violent, never articulate except for strong half-words that the noise of the engine did not drown. He was driven by the maddening isolation of this to go and stand at the foot of the hatchway, and one by one peel the potatoes there. If Gregson's order were to be taken literally he would peel about forty of them. He stood there looking up into the shaft of sea-light, peeling his fifteenth potato, when Jimmy came sliding down the hatch without any warning except a violent and wordless sort of bellow. The boy watched him disappear into the tiny and confined engine-cradle that was not big enough to be called a room, and then bawled after him: "What's up, Jimmy? What's up now?"

"Somebody in the sea!" Jimmy said.

The boy went up the hatchway with a half-peeled potato still in his hands. The engine died behind him as he went, and Jimmy followed him a moment later.

On deck Gregson and the pilot were up in the bows. Gregson was lumbering about in a state of heavy excitement. The pilot seemed, to the boy coming up into the sharp winter sunlight out of the gloom of the cabin, about seven feet tall and crowned by a crumpled hat of coffee-brown fur. He was at that moment about to pull his flying jacket over his head. The sharp released pressure of it shocked the wide moustache into a dishevelment that was for some reason more serious than even its bushy correctitude had been. The pilot took off his white under-sweater, and then began to take off his boots. He seemed to hesitate about his thick grey under-socks and then decided to take them off too. "Is he still coming in?" he said to Gregson; and Gregson, leaning heavily over the side bawled, "He's floatin' on his back. He's a Jerry all right too."

"Yes, he's a Jerry all right," the pilot said, and stood ready, side by side with Gregson and the boy, watching about sixty feet away the floating and feebly propelling body of a man awkwardly moving across the face of the sea like a puffing yellow crab.

"Want a line?" Gregson said.

"Want a line?" the young man said. "I could swim to France."

He went over the side a moment later in a smooth and careless dive that took him under and brought him up, fifteen or twenty feet away, with the shaking howl of a dog having fun. He began to strike out with strokes of deep power, turning backward with each of them a moustache that looked suddenly as if it had been pasted on to the strong wet face. All the fancy oddities of the man became in those few moments washed away. He seemed to be feeling forward to grasp the solid fabric of the sea so that he could tear it with his hands. He reached the other man, now moving with spidery feebleness parallel to the boat, in about twenty seconds, and rolled over beside him, coming up a moment later underneath and slightly to one side. The blue sleeve of his arm came up across the yellow inflated German life-jacket, and then sleeve and jacket and the yellowish heads of both men began to move towards the boat together.

The boy stood fascinated. Every now and then Gregson, huge and majestic, pushed his body a foot or two along the boatside, moving in time with the swimming pilot and at the same time pushing the boy along with him too. The boy was sometimes half-obliterated by the bulk of Gregson, and

Gregson in turn was impeded by the boy. Neither of them seemed to notice it.

The curiosity of the boy was so intense that it almost blinded him. The blob of yellow and blue coming in towards the boat sometimes receded and was lost for a second or two like an illusion. When it reappeared it seemed gigantic. The boy could then see clearly the water-flattened moustache of the pilot every time the head was thrown back, and he could see the upper half of the body of the rescued man. It seemed quite lifeless. But suddenly as it came nearer the boy could see lying across the chest of it a leather strap. It was attached to a leather case that appeared every second or so from below the sea and then was lost again. The boy in a moment of painful and speechless joy knew what it was.

At that same moment Gregson, excited too, flattened him against the boatside so that he could not move. And since he could not move Gregson could not move either, and Gregson in that moment became aware of him again.

"What the pipe, Snowy! Git out on it!" Gregson bawled. "Git down and git some tea! They'll want it. Go on. Git crackin'! Git that tea."

With a curve of his hand Gregson hooked the boy from the boatside. It was a sort of friendly blow and it took the boy across the deck and down the narrow hatchway and into the cabin below before he was aware of it.

He stood there for some moments in an excited stupor before realizing that he still had in his hands a half-peeled potato. It had on it the oily imprint of his fingers where he had clenched it. As he stood holding it he heard Gregson bawling on deck. He tried to hear what Gregson was saying, but the words were confused and he got the impression only of mighty, exciting events overhead.

This impression exploded his stupor. He was filled with violent energy. His head rocked with the astonishing possibilities of the leather case slung across the body of the German, and he ached to be part of the world of men.

He put fresh tea into the teapot with his hands and then poured water on it and found two extra cups in the locker by the stove. Nothing like this had ever happened before: no pilot, no rescue, no Jerry, no binoculars. He heard Gregson shouting again: this time much louder, something about a gun. The boy, standing with head upraised, listening, was swept by a torrent of new possibilities. Back in the pub, at home, there were boys with the luck of the gods. They owned sections of air cannon-guns, belts of unfired cartridges. He suddenly saw before him the wonder of incredible chances. He did not know what happened to the guns and binoculars of dead pilots or even captured pilots, but now, at last, he was going to know.

He poured tea into the two cups and was in the act of stirring sugar into them when he heard, from overhead, two new sounds. Somebody was running across the deck, and from a south-easterly direction, faint but to him clear enough, came the sound of a plane. He did not connect these sounds. He had momentarily lost interest in the sound of aircraft. Something much more exciting was happening on deck. Gregson was shouting again, and again there was the sound of feet running across the deck. They were so heavy that he thought perhaps they were Gregson's feet. But it was all very confused and exciting, and he had no time to disentangle the sound of voices from the sound of feet and the rising sound of the now not so distant plane. Nor did it matter very much. He had in that moment reached the fine and rapid conclusion that war was wonderful.

He picked up a cup of tea in each hand. He turned to walk out of the galley when he was arrested suddenly by the near violence of the plane. It was coming towards *The Breadwinner* very fast and very low. The roar of it obliterated the last of the voices on deck. It turned the sound of feet into an echo. He ran out of the galley with the tea in his hands and had reached the bottom step of the gangway when he heard the strangest sound of all. It was the sound of the Lewis gun being fired.

It fired for perhaps half a second and then stopped. He did not know how he knew the difference between this sound and the sound of cannon firing directly afterwards and for about two seconds from overhead, but he sprawled down the steps on his face. The scalding tea poured down his arms, up the sleeve of his jacket and down his chest, but it did not seem hot and there was no pain. He did not look upward, but he felt the square of light at the head of the gangway darkened out for the space of a second as the plane went overhead. He was sure for one moment that the plane would hit the deck but the moment passed, and then the plane itself passed, and there was no more firing, either from the deck or overhead. And at last, when the plane had gone, there was no more sound.

He waited for what seemed a long time before crawling up the gangway. He pulled himself up by his hands because his legs did not seem part of him. The small auxiliary of *The Breadwinner* had stopped and now it was dead silent everywhere.

THE BOY BROUGHT TO THE SCENE ON DECK A KIND OF ghastly unbelief. For a moment or two he could not stand up. He lay with his head resting on the top step of the gangway, and became for some seconds quite sightless, as if he had stared at the sun. Shadowy and crimson lumps of something floated in front of him like bits of coloured cloud and then solidified, gradually, into a single object across the deck. The boy lay there staring infinitely at this thing. It had about it something he distantly recognized. It was like a shapeless bundle of sea-blue cloth tied about the middle with lengths of slate-crimson rubber hose. It was some time before the boy brought himself to understand that this bundle had once been Jimmy, and that the tangle of hose was all that remained of the guts of the gunner-engineer.

He got up at last and walked away, forward, up the deck. All the forward part of the boat was hidden from him by the deck-house. He suddenly felt alone on the ship. And now as he walked he also got the impression of being verylarge but that the ship was also very large and that consequently he could never reach the end of it. He wanted to shout for Gregson. He felt the air very cold on his face and colder still on his chest and arms, where the tea had spilled, and then still colder on his eyes, shocked stiff by what he had seen of the engineer. This coldness became suddenly the frantic substance of a new terror. It was as if he had something alive and deadly in his hands and wanted to drop it.

He began to run. He ran like a blind man, away from something, careless completely of all that lay before him. As he ran past the deck-house he began jabbering incoherent and violent words that were partly his fear and partly something to do with the need for telling someone of his fantastic discoveries. For the first time he had seen the dead.

He ran in reality about two yards beyond the deck-house. The fear that had driven him forward from behind seemed to have got round in front of him, and now slapped him in the face. It stopped him abruptly. And as he stopped the coherence of his speech came back with perfect shrillness. He was shouting "Jimmy! Jimmy! Jimmy! Jimmy!" in a cry that was somewhere between anguish and a refusal to believe.

When this was over he looked down on the deck. It seemed very overcrowded with the figures that lay there. They were the figures of the young pilot and the German, who lay side by side, together, and then of Gregson, who was lying half across them.

The boy gazed for some seconds at the bodies of the three men. They lay in the attitudes of men who had been playfully wrestling. There was something quiet and merciful in the tangle of limbs and there was no blood and he could see the moustache of the young pilot plastered down by sea-water on his face like the moustache of a comedian. He was very convinced of their being dead.

Out of all this there emerged, suddenly, something very wonderful. He saw the enormous body of Gregson, on its hands and knees, heaving itself slowly upward, and then he realized several things. He realized that he was fantastically fond of the living Gregson, and he realized too that he must have run up from the galley and across the deck, in the silence after the shots were fired, in the space of a second or two. He caught for the first time the sound of the plane, quite loud still, receding across the sea.

"Mr. Gregson, Mr. Gregson, Captain, Captain, Captain, Captain, Captain, Skipper!" he said. "Skipper!"

"Snowy," Gregson said. He swung himself slowly round in the attitude of an elephant kneeling and looked up at the boy blinking. "Rum 'un," he said. "Where was you?"

The boy found that he could not speak. He wanted to tell of Jimmy. He made small, frantic and almost idiotic gestures with his mouth and hands.

"Hadn' half got some cheek, hadn' he?" Gregson said. "The sod."

It seemed to the boy that Gregson was concerned with frivolous commentaries. He still had the weight of impalpable terrors on his mind. Gregson, still on his hands and knees, groped forward like a man blinded by daylight. "You all right, kid?" he said. "All right y'self, eh?"

"Jimmy," the boy said. "Jimmy!"

"I heard him firing that bleedin' thing. Wonder as it fired, first time. Like the bleedin' injun."

On the deck the young pilot began suddenly to mutter repeated groans of agony, trying to turn himself over.

The sound and the movement woke Gregson out of himself. He crawled between the two pilots and leaned over the English one. "All right," he said. "All right? Where'd it git y'?" The young man was trying to push his heels through the deck, lifting his body with recurrent convulsions of pain. "The bastards, the bastards!" Gregson said. He turned and spoke to the German pilot, lying half on his side with his knees against his chest. "Bleedin' low flying. Is that the sort a bleedin' orders you git?" There was no reply except a violent convulsive jerk that threw the German down on his face.

"Christ," the English boy said. "Christ."

He turned and looked up at the sky, rolling his head quietly from side to side. His face in colour was something like the sea, blue-grey and lightless and very cold. Flecks of sea-water, like sweat, were still gathered on the grey skin of the forehead, and his body was still soaked from swimming so that the clothes were shrivelled on it.

"I'll git you down below," Gregson said.

"Don't move me," the pilot said. "Don't move me."

"Better down below. Git you warm. Git y' in a bunk. I can carry you."

"No," the pilot said. "Don't move me. It's wrong. Cover me over. Cover me over, that's all."

He rolled his head in spasms of recurrent agony from side to side as he spoke. "Git them blankets, Snowy," Gregson said. "All on 'em. And the first-aid box. And tell Jimmy to come for-ard. Soon's he can."

The boy went down to the cabin in cold daze of fright made worse by a determination not to look at Jimmy. He was hypnotized by the bloody tangle of flesh, crushed to the livid shapelessness of rejected offal, that lay on the deck, and he could not pass it without looking that way. The sight of it drove him below with wild energy. When he came up again, carrying the grey bundle of blankets, in a trembling terror of fresh sickness, he determined this time not to look. But now as he passed he saw that Jimmy held something in his hands. It was the handle of the Lewis gun, severed from the rest of the frying-pan apparatus by the same curious miracle that had kept it in Jimmy's hands. It was painted harshly with coagulations of new blood.

It was the thought of Jimmy that kept him standing for some seconds by the side of Gregson, holding the blankets and not speaking. Gregson was kneeling between the two pilots. The German was now turned over, on his back, and was revealed also to be very young, drained of colour and in pain. He was moaning slightly, as if talking to himself, weakly throwing back his fair head. He was perhaps nineteen; he looked to the boy to be like the Englishman, wonderfully and terribly worn by the experience of battles. Pain had beaten deep hollows in his cheeks, so that the facial bone everywhere stood out, the skin white and polished where it had tightened.

But it was not this that fascinated the boy. He now found himself staring at the binoculars Gregson had unlooped and laid on the deck. It was clear now that they were binoculars; he had never seen anything that seemed so magnificent. They lay on the deck just above the German's head, the light-brown leather dark and salty with sea-water, the initials K.M. in black on the side. Gazing at them, the boy forgot the figure of the engineer lying in the attitude of discarded offal in the stern.

Gregson took the blankets out of his arms as he stood there staring down at the leather case. He said something about "Ah, thassa boy, Snowy," but the boy did not really hear. He stood watching Gregson cover over first the English pilot and then the German, giving them three blankets each. A little wind had sprung up from the southwest and caught one of the blankets and blew it away from the German's feet. The boy bent down and pushed the feet back under the blanket and the German screamed with pain.

The boy stood back in fear and guilt, as if he had really done something to cause this agony. He could not speak. Gregson comforted the German with words that were simply neutral whispers that even the boy did not understand.

It astonished both Gregson and the boy to hear the German break the silence after the scream and say, quite quietly: "I think it is my leg. I think it is both my legs perhaps."

"Speaks English!" Gregson said. It was less a comment than a statement of wonder: as if it were very remarkable that somebody of another nation should know Gregson's language. "English! Speaks English!"

"I think it is my leg," the German said.

"I ain't much at fust aid," Gregson said. "But we'll keep you warm. Git you back ashore. Quick. See? Hospital. See?"

"I didn't bring the first-aid box up," Snowy said. "I forgot."

No one seemed to notice this remark, and the English boy said, "How long before we can get in?"

"Depends," Gregson said. "Hour or more. Depends if the engineer can hot it up."

The boy stood rigid. His mind was in an anxiety of explosive intentions. It was his duty to tell Gregson that Jimmy would never hot it up again.

"Git some tea, Snowy," Gregson said. "Some brandy ain't they, too? Put some o' that in. Four mugs. You have some brandy too. No, five. You'll want one for Jimmy too."

"Jimmy——"

"Go on, bring it up smart. Five mugs, Snowy boy." He looked with powerful expansiveness and anger at the sky. "I wonder where that sod went? I thought Jimmy'd got him," so that for a moment the boy thought he was threatening him.

"He certainly made mincemeat of us," the English boy said.

"I'd mincemeat the bastard," Gregson said. "Next time I'll have that gun. Jimmy!"

The violence of this shout drove the boy in fear from the deck and haunted him with constant terror as he made tea in the galley below. His movements were automatic and thoughtless in the little cabin between the bunks. He did not need any processes of deduction to know what he might expect when he went on deck again.

This time he put the mugs of tea on an iron tray, so that he could carry them in a single journey. He had filled them up with brandy. And for some reason he could not bear to go with four mugs only and not five, and so there were five, as if he thought the presence of the fifth would have some effect on the fact of death.

He carried the tray on deck and became aware, for the first time since the shooting, what change had come over the day. Low cloud had begun to come up from the west, in misty waves that had already in them a light spray of grey rain, and there was no light, except far eastward, on the face of the sea.

The position of Gregson on the deck had something at once awful and inevitable about it. It did not surprise the boy. It appeared fantastically exact. He stood a yard or two from where the gun had once been, legs apart, arms stiff and outwardly stretched down. It was only the colour of these arms that shocked the boy; they were bright with blood. But where the body of Jimmy had been lying like a brutally rejected heap of smashed flesh there was now only a brown tarpaulin. It had not even the remembered shape of the dead man.

Gregson looked at the boy as he came up with the tea. He was wiping the blood from his hands with a piece of engine rag. It seemed to the boy that his enormity had about it a shocked kindliness.

"Won't want five cups, Snowy," he said.

"I know," the boy said. He wanted to cry. "I saw it." He spoke of the engineer impersonally, in fear and respect.

"Got three kids," Gregson said. He stood with his vast body broken and deflated by thoughts of Jimmy. "Nice job. Nice thing." He wiped his hands with the oily rag, until the fingers were a dull brown from the mixing of blood and oil. "He allus wanted to fire that gun. Allus wanted to fire it. Well, he fired it," he said, as if, perhaps, this thought would atone for all that was done.

"Better take the tea along," he said, "while it's hot. Looks like rain."

The boy went forward with the tea, past the deck-house, to where the two pilots were lying together. He heard Gregson behind him swirling his hands in a bucket of water. The two pilots were talking to each other and the binoculars lay on the deck.

"Damn funny thing," the English boy was saying. "All the time I had an idea it was you."

"I don't think it was so funny."

"Teach you not to come fooling over on these low-level jobs, anyway," the Englishman said. "There's no future in that."

They were both smiling.

"I got some tea," Snowy said.

"Good show." The English boy tried to lift his head, and relapsed in a paroxysm of pain that seemed to twist his entire spine. "God!" he said. "God!" He lay breathing deeply, his lips trembling. "God, oh God."

Gregson came up and leaned over him. To the boy his hands were white as paper. He had never seen them so clean. Gregson laid them quietly on the English boy's shoulders.

"You take it easy. I may have to get you below after all. Looks like rain. Smoke?"

"I don't," the boy said. "Perhaps Jerry does. His name's Karl Messner. Flies Messerschmitts. Should say flew Messerschmitts."

"I don't care if he flew bloody archangels," Gregson said. "He's gittin' no fags o' mine."

"He understands English."

"He does, does he? Well, bloody good job too. That makes it clear. He knows what I'm thinking."

"Ah, go on. He's the sod I shot down. The one I told you about."

"Is he? Pity his guts wasn't shot out. Like Jimmy's. The engineer. You saw him. Him with the gun."

Gregson looked from one of the pilots to the other, and then to the boy, in a single fierce glance of challenge to all of them. They did not speak. The German lay with eyes fixed upward, as if he were trying not to hear it all.

"Yeh, Jimmy's dead," Gregson said. "They bust him up all right."

The English pilot looked as if he were going to shake his head, and then, remembering the earlier pain, thought better of it, simply opening his eyes and shutting them again.

"I'm sorry," he said. "But he didn't do it. He's not the type. You give him tea, anyway. What's the odds?"

"Ah, all right," Gregson said. "Go on. What's the odds? That's right. What's the odds? What's it matter? What's it matter now?" He furiously threw his cigarette packet and matches across to the German.

They lay on the German's chest. He did not pick them up.

Gregson seized bitterly on this significant fact, making much of it. "Too proud to take 'em, anyway. Lower your bloody self to give 'em all you got and then they bleedin' insult you. Makes me sick." He threw about him fresh challenges, now doubly embittered.

"Pull your finger out, Jerry," the English boy said. "No sulking. Take the captain's cigarettes when he offers them."

The German did not move.

"The Captain wants to throw you overboard. He hates Germans. There's nobody to stop him either if he wants to."

The English boy was having fun; his face had a kind of sad sideways grin on it as he spoke. But the German did not move.

"Throw him overboard, Captain," the English boy said. "I shan't tell."

"All right," the German said. He moved his hands to the cigarettes. "Thank you very much. Very kind of you. Thank you very much."

"All that bleedin' fuss for nothing," Gregson said.

"Behave yourself, Messner old boy," the Englishman said. "You're just a P.O.W. now."

The boy, listening to all this, felt the tremendous impact of the more serious, more curious, more important world of men. He set cups of tea down on the deck, one each by the pilots and one for Gregson. He took one for himself and left the odd one on the tray. This odd cup did not now impress him by its forlorn significance, nor any longer as being part of the dead engineer. He saw that there were attitudes in which it was possible to make light of pain, to be jocular about the impact of death. And part of the terror about Jimmy now receded in his mind.

"I don't think I can sit up," the English boy said. "Bad show."

"I'll hold you," Gregson said.

"No," the boy said. "Better give it to me in the spoon."

While Gregson cautiously lifted the English boy's head and held it slightly upward with one hand and then spoon-fed tea to him with the other, the German raised himself on one elbow. He held cigarette and tea-cup in the same hand, turning his face away and looking westward over the sea. He appeared to the boy as a person of sinister and defiant quality. The boy read into his silence, his gaze over the sea, and the way he let his cigarette burn away without smoking it, a meditation on escape. He hoped that he would escape. If he escaped, Gregson would kill him. That would be a wonderful thing. If he were killed the boy would take the binoculars. That would be another wonderful thing. And when at last he reached home he would wear them slung on his shoulder, taking with him some of that same defiant quality of the man who returns with the trophies of war.

It began to rain as he stood there watching the German, the spits fine and dark and quite fast, wetting the deck. Gregson lifted his face to the sky. "All appearance on it," he said. "Better git you below."

On the face of the English boy there was a curious sort of pain. It crumpled the youthful texture of his face, making it very old. It did not occur to the boy Snowy that it might be a look of fear. He did not even remotely connect fear with men.

"Get Messner down," the English boy said, grinning suddenly. "Guests first."

"You're a caution you are," Gregson said.

"Get him down."

"I'll have you both down in two shakes."

"Well, get him down first. If you drop him I'll know what to do."

Very gently Gregson let the English boy's head lie back on the deck. "Snowy'll stay with you," he said. Grinning, he seemed suddenly moved, for some reason, to extravagant praises of the boy. "Masterpiece of a kid for aircraft. Knows 'em all."

"Good show," the pilot said. "Good old Snowy." He smiled at the boy.

Gregson went over to the German, put both arms under his back and began to lift him. There was something cruelly odd about the German's legs. They seemed to have an existence independent of the rest of his body. Gregson became aware that if he lifted him the legs would simply hang down, powerless, like lumps of loose rubber. He heard the German gasping deeply for breath.

Gregson laid him back on the deck. "Easy," he said. "Easy. We'll git the stretcher."

It was raining quite fast now, but the German, lying rigidly back, staring upward and swallowing his breath in rain and heavy gasps of pain, seemed glad to receive it on his face. He opened his lips, and as the drops fell into his mouth he licked them in relief with his tongue.

The stretcher was kept lashed to one side of the narrow skylight lying aft of the hatchway. Gregson unfastened it and carried it along the deck under one arm. "Job for you, Snowy," he said, "mind your backside."

The space on deck seemed more than ever confined; the stretcher had something of the effect of a ladder brought into a tiny room. Gregson laid the stretcher on deck, parallel with the German, and in a moment the boy was on his knees, undoing the straps.

The boy stood by while Gregson lifted the shoulders of the German on to the stretcher. He saw the German clenching his hands. "Please," he said. "Please. My legs." Gregson did not speak, but slowly slid the legs across to the stretcher too. In this moment the German threw his hands violently upward and brought them down with a savage double slap on his own face, keeping them tightly there in frantic self–created pain, sobbing with quiet terror underneath his white fingers. The boy was less affected by this, an outburst of crying from the adult enemy, than by the mess of blood that smeared the deck where the German's legs had been.

The German kept his hands crushed down on his face while Gregson and the boy carried him below on the stretcher, Gregson taking the weight of the stretcher by going first, the boy struggling slowly behind down the narrow steps. They laid him on the cabin floor between the bunks. The boy set down his end of the stretcher with a certain air of expansive and careless pride; it was the first time he had taken part in such things. He stood erect and regarded Gregson and the German with tired gravity, languidly rubbing his hands together. He was no longer aware of the shock of seeing blood for the second time. He was elevated into a world of catastrophe and pain, bringing to it a taut and suppressed excitement.

The German still had his hands pressed over his face as Gregson and the boy went back on deck, Gregson carrying the stretcher. Not even the pain of being moved from the stretcher to the floor of the cabin had had any effect on them. He used them all the time to contain and conceal the agony of his face.

On deck it was raining quite fast. The English boy had covered his face with the blankets, and lay rigid and entirely hidden by them, like a corpse. As Gregson and the boy arrived with the stretcher he sharply uncovered his face, grinned stiffly up at them with a face of pale bone-shadows that did nothing to lessen that effect. "Collect up my things," he said to the boy, "the things I took off. Before they get soaked," and the boy went forward with proud obedience to where the pilot had kicked off his boots and socks on the deck.

When he had gone Gregson leaned over the pilot. "Can you move?" he said. "A little bit. Just slide over while I take the weight?"

"How's old Messner?" the boy said. "Did you drop him?"

"Now," Gregson said. "Just gently. While I hold you."

"God!" the boy said. "God. Oh! Jesus, Jesus." He cried gently through his lips while he held them clenched with his teeth, and the rain poured fast and heavy on his face and on the light hair already wet with sea, so that his whole appearance was strangely wild and battered. Suddenly Gregson threw the blanket over his face, and then, just as the boy came back with the flying boots and socks, lifted him bodily, in a single smooth but desperate movement, on to the stretcher. In that attitude, covered over and silent and never moving, the pilot lay on the stretcher while Gregson and the boy carried him below, the rain quickening heavily on the south-west wind and turning already to lighter and thinner crimson the lumps of blood about the deck.

It was about five minutes before the boy reappeared on deck, coming to collect the tray and the five cups still half-filled with tea. This time he did not look at the covered heap that had once been the engineer, and the blood where the two pilots had lain did not have on him any more effect than the blood he often saw on the floor of the fish-market behind the quay.

He was thinking only of the binoculars. The case was very wet from sea-water, and he had some difficulty in getting them out. He pulled at them until the suction of water in the case was released, and then when he had them out he stood up on deck and looked through them, across the sea and through the grey and driving mass of rain.

For some reason or other, either because the sea-water had reached the lenses or because the lenses themselves were not adjusted for his sight, what he saw through the glasses was only a grey and misty mass of unproportioned light. It had no relation to the things the had expected.

Trembling, he hastily put the glasses back into the case and gathered up the cups and hurried below, lowering his head against the darting rain.

DOWN BELOW A NEW PROBLEM HAD ARISEN. HE WAS startled by Gregson's voice muttering crustily from the box where Jimmy had so often been lost among the miseries of the auxiliary:

"Know anything about injuns, Snowy?"

The boy put the tea-tray and the binoculars on the cabin table, on either side of which the two pilots lay rigidly on the floor. The English boy had closed his eyes and the German did not look at the binoculars.

He went back to Gregson. Gregson, unable to squeeze himself into the hole containing the engine, was squatting half in and half out of it, regarding the engine with melancholy helplessness and slowly wiping it with an oil rag, as if in some way this would make it go.

"I know you turn the bleedin' handle, and that's all I do know."

"Ought to be simple," the boy said, "if I can get it set."

"Wouldn't let nobody look at it," Gregson said. His grievances against Jimmy were not yet quite extinguished. "Wouldn't let nobody touch it. Kept it to 'isself. Wust on it." He stopped wiping the engine and let the oily rag rest heavily on it, shaking his head. "Wust on it. Allus knew best. You couldn't talk to him!"

There flashed across the boy's mind an image of Jimmy lying redly disembowelled on the deck, unrecognisable and shapeless, and he said quickly:

"You switch her on down here, I know that."

"Ah, go on then. You do it."

Gregson moved his huge body a foot or two backwards. This action gave the boy a sudden sense of space. He could move with astonishing freedom in the dark space among the gears. He became aware also of carrying a sense of responsibility arising from a succession of terrific events: the presence and sight of death, the fact of the binoculars, the business of carrying the wounded pilots below, and now the engine. He had come to think of the engine as sacred. It was not to be touched; it belonged to Jimmy; its faults and secrets were part of the man.

He squeezed himself in alongside the cradle and pressed the needle of the carburettor up and down, flooding it. He had watched Jimmy do these things. The engine was a mass of odd lengths of wire, strange extra gadgets devised by Jimmy, so that it had the look of an unfinished invention. One of these wires held the choke. It was necessary to pull it out, hook it back into fixed position by means of a piece of cord that slipped over a nail in the cradle, and only release it when the engine was running too fast. You turned her over twice before switching on.

Gregson, watching the boy do these things, said in a curious whisper:

"We gotta git back fast. You know that, don't you?"

The boy nodded. It occurred to him suddenly that he had no idea of what had happened on deck.

"He was so bleedin' low," Gregson said, "you could have touched his wings. I thought he was goin' to cut me head off. Firing like blazes all the time too. Mowed us down. We was like heap o' bloody dogs on a bone when he'd gone." He looked over his shoulder for a second. "Know they're both hit bad, don't ye'? You know that?"

The boy nodded and said he thought he could get her started now. Gregson stood back a little and the boy, with a sort of careless strength, pressed his weight down on the starting handle with his right hand. "Think you can match it?" Gregson said. The boy answered with something that was very near to tired contempt. "Can't start first time. You gotta get her swung over."

"Oh! that's it, is it?" Gregson said. He was fond of telling the boy that he had been brought up in sail. In fact, he had never been brought up in sail. He had always known engines of some sort, mostly old and mostly small and mostly, if he looked back, nothing but trouble. He had never trusted them. And he had suddenly the conviction that he trusted them less than ever now. He stood with his hands spread with large uneasiness over his belly. It was very quiet everywhere except for the sound of rain beating with a hard murmur on the deck; a sound for some reason irritating and unfriendly, so that suddenly he wondered what time it was.

He had not time to pull his watch out of his trousers pocket before the boy had swung the handle of the engine over, and he forgot the watch in his surprise. It did not surprise him that the engine did not fire; he was used to that; but only that the boy had succeeded in swinging it with exactly the knack of the dead engineer. The boy had learnt by heart the ways of the dead man, and the sudden repetition of them seemed to bring him in a curious way back to life, so that he seemed to be there with them in the absurd and dirty little engine-hole, his face dark with pessimism and long-suffering with pain.

By the time the boy had swung the engine the fourth time Gregson was sour with the conviction that it was never going to fire. The boy leaned his weight on the cylinder head, panting: "No spark in her," he said. He desired passionately to make the engine go, feeling that in doing so he would become in Gregson's eyes a sort of adult hero. But there was something queer about the engine. "No compression there," he said.

"Compression, compression!" Gregson said. "Let me have a go." He had not the faintest idea what compression was. He seized the engine-handle rather as if it had been the key of a clock. When he swung it finally it swirled round, under his immense strength, two or three complete revolutions, swinging him off his balance against the bulkhead.

"Bloody thing never was no good!" he said. "Allus said so. Told him. Miracle it ever went." He leaned against the bulkhead panting in savage and heavy despair.

The boy did not answer. He was crawling back into the dark recesses behind the engine-cradle, where there was just room enough for him to kneel. He did not know quite what he was looking for. Underneath the engine block lay pools of spent oil in which he knelt as he crawled. It suddenly occurred to him that these pools were too large. He put down his right hand and knew that they were pools of oil and water. Then he stopped crawling and began to run his hands over the engine-block until he found the place where cannon shell had ripped it open in a single jagged hole. A little oil still clogged it there. The force of the shell had lifted up the head, warping it as it blew.

The boy called back to Gregson. From the dark interior Gregson seemed to fill the entire space below the gangway, and it suddenly struck the boy that it was a miracle that he, so large a thing in a little ship, had not been hit.

"We've had it," he said.

"Had what?" Gregson said. "Whadya mean? What's up?"

The boy crawled out of the hole, suddenly tired, his knees and hands black with oil which he wiped thoughtlessly over his face and in streaks across his almost white hair.

"We've had the engine," the boy said. "That's what. Cannon shell."

Gregson lifted his enormous face, swelling the creases of his great neck until they were blown with anger.

"Why'n't they bleedin' well sink us? Why'n't they bleedin' well sink us and have done?"

The boy, hearing the wind rising now with the sound of rain on deck, was sharply aware of a new crisis.

"What do we do now?" he said. He was aware that things might, without the engine, be very tough, very desperate. He licked his lips and tasted the sickliness of oil on them. "What do we do now?"

"Gitta us a cuppa tea," Gregson roared. "Gitta us a cuppa tea!"

He bawled and raged up the companionway into the beating rain.

THE ENGLISH PILOT OPENED HIS EYES WITH A SHARP blink, as if he had been lost in a dream and the boy had startled him out of it into the cramped and gloomy world of the little cabin. Messner still lay with eyes closed, his face turned away. The only light in the cabin was from a single skylight, about a yard square, of opaque glass, over which rain had already thrown a deeper film. In this iron-grey light the pilot looked on the boy as he might have looked on a shape moulded vaguely out of the shadows: as something that moved and had the tangibility of a face, but as otherwise without identity. He regarded the boy also as if there was nothing he could do or wanted to do to change or sharpen his shadowiness. His eyes had dropped deeper into the bruised sockets of his face. As they gazed upwards and followed with reactions that were never quite swift enough the movements of the boy they had on them the same lightless film as the skylight above.

It was some time before he could see clearly enough through the stupor of weakness to grasp that the boy was busy with an object that looked like a torch. This torch, though the boy held it upwards, towards the skylight, and downwards and sideways, towards himself and Messner, never seemed to light. He expected it to flash into his face, but after the boy had swivelled it round two or three times he found himself dazed by angry irritation against it. It became part of the pain buried centrally, like a deep hammer blow, just above his eyes and extending, in a savage cord, to the base of his spine.

"What the hell are you doing?" he said.

The boy was surprised not by the abruptness of the voice but by its softness. It seemed like a voice from a long way off. It made him feel slightly guilty.

"Not much," he said.

"Put that torch down," the pilot said. "Don't wave it about."

"Not a torch," the boy said. "Pair of glasses."

"Glasses?"

"Binoculars. The German's. I found them on deck."

"Oh," the pilot said.

"Can't make them work," the boy said. "Everything looks wrong."

"Let me look at them," the pilot said. "They ought to be good, German binoculars."

He held his hands upward, weakly, without extending his arms, and the boy bent down and gave him the glasses. He let them lie on his chest for some moments and the boy saw it heaving deeply, as if the movement of reaching for the glasses had exhausted him. It seemed quite a long time before he slowly lifted them to his face. Then when he held them there it was without doing anything with them. His hands did not move on the adjustment screws. He rested the eyepieces lightly against the deep sockets of his eyes and simply held them there without a word, in what seemed a dream of tiredness or forgetfulness or pain. It did not occur to the boy that there might be in this long and silent inertia a savage struggle to behave with decent normality, without fuss, to accomplish the simple task of revolving the screws and say something about it without the shadow of even a small agony.

After some longer interval the pilot let the glasses rest slowly back on his chest. To the boy it seemed that he grasped them with extraordinary tightness. He gave a worried sort of smile. It was very quiet and strengthless, but quite calm, and seemed as if it were intended to be reassuring.

"Needs adjustment, that's all," he said. His words were hard, gasped out quickly. "I can do it. Quite easy. Nice pair."

He held the glasses hard against his chest and stared straight beyond the boy with a sort of lost vehemence. His eyes seemed to have difficulty in focussing on some point in very obscure and difficult distance far beyond the varnished pitch-pine walls of the cabin. They were terribly desperate.

But what worried the boy was that the glasses were held also with this same rigid desperation. He waited for some moments for the pilot to give them back to him. Then it became clear that they were not coming back. The pilot grasped them still harder against the blankets which covered him and then shut his eyes.

The boy stood gazing down for some moments, troubled and waiting for something to happen. Suddenly he knew that he was forgotten. It was no use. He remembered the tea. He took a last look at the figure of the pilot lying absolutely still and rigid, grasping the binoculars as he had sometimes seen dying men in pictures grasping a cross, and then pushed the kettle on to the galley fire. He poured the stale cold tea out of the dirty cups into the slop bucket by the galley. He was sick of tea; he was sick of a succession of daily crises in all of which Gregson demanded tea, only to let it get cold without drinking it, and then demanded still more tea as another crisis created itself, letting it get cold again. He jangled the half-dirty cups together on the table, banging them against the pan of peeled potatoes.

About this time Messner turned on his back and began to moan. His lips were very blue and dry but his eyes were not open, so that it seemed as though he were turning and crying in his sleep. The boy heard him with something between sickness and indifference, and ignored him for some moments with callousness. He had made up his mind that the only virtue in Messner was that he owned the binoculars. He regarded him at the same time with a certain distant awe. Messner was an enemy; so that even though you had never seen him before in your life he was a wrong, criminal, despicably cruel, dynamically dangerous person. It was men like Messner who came in low over the sand-dunes, the sea-marshes and the little towns of the coast, using cannon-shell at low range on whatever living thing they could find. There was no doubt about that; the boy had seen it happen. It was perfectly acceptable that Messner was no different from the rest of them; but when after a time Messner ceased moaning for an interval and lay rigid on his back and staring upward with quiet lips there did not seem very much difference in the appearance of the two men lying on the floor.

Reluctantly making fresh tea at last, the boy remembered that he ought to call Gregson. He went to the bottom of the companionway and shouted, "Mr. Gregson, skipper, tea!" But there was no movement and no answering shout above the sound of rain. Also, as he looked upward and saw the rain flicking in steady white drizzle across the section of dark sky, he felt there was something odd about *The Breadwinner*, and when he had taken two or three steps up the companionway he saw what it was. He saw that Gregson had rigged a sail. The boy went slowly on deck and marvelled at this strange copper-brown triangle with a sort of reluctant wonder. He had never seen it before. It gave to the dumpy, war-painted *Breadwinner* an exciting loftiness; it made her seem a larger ship. It even seemed to dwarf the enormous figure of Gregson, pressing his belly rather harder than usual against the wheel, the peak of his cap rather harder down on his head.

"Tea, Mr. Gregson," the boy said. "Just made."

"Ain't got time!" Gregson roared at him.

The boy stood in the attitude of someone stunned on his feet; he was more shocked than he had been by the sight of the dead engineer. He stared at the face of Gregson pressing itself forward with a sort of pouted savagery against the driving rain, eyes popped forward, chin sunk hard into doubled and redoubled folds of inflamed flesh on the collar of his jersey. It was some moments before he could think of anything to say.

"Just ready," he said at last. It did not seem remotely credible that Gregson could reject tea. "I can bring it up."

"Ain't got time I tell yer!" Gregson said. "Ain't got time for nothing. That wind's gittin' up. Look at that sea too! Look at it! We gotta git them chaps in."

The boy turned and saw, for the first time since the shooting, what had happened to the weather. Rain and wind beating up the Channel had already ploughed the sea into shallow and ugly troughs of foam. The distances had narrowed in, so that the skyline was no longer divisible from the smoky and shortened space of sea. Overhead he saw lumpy masses of rain-cloud skidding north-eastward. "Another hour and it'll blow your guts out!" Gregson said. "We went too far west. I knowed it." He had nursed the old superstitions in his mind, placing them against events. The boy remembered the desperate sarcasms of the dead Jimmy, appealing for a second auxiliary, but he said nothing. It was too late now.

"You git below," Gregson said, "and look after them two."

"Yes."

"Well, don't stand there!"

The boy was startled by the fury of Gregson's words and turned instantly and went back to the companionway. As he did so he saw the covered heap of the dead engineer's body, blackened now with rain, the blood washed into diluted and glistening blotches of crimson on the wet deck, and this forlorn heap of deathliness that somehow still did not seem dead brought back suddenly all the chaos and terror of the thing, all the nearness and all the pain. He went below in a cold black sweat and stood at the table and poured himself tea and drank it in hot violent gulps of relief. The boat had begun to sway a little, in short brisk lurches, still shallow. Already they were increasing and he knew they would not stop now. Soon she would pitch forward too, and if the wind rose enough she would fall into the regular violence of double pitch and roll that would not cease until she was within half a mile of shore.

The tea did something to dispel the horror of memory. He drained the cup before becoming aware that other things were happening in the cabin.

The English pilot had stretched out one hand until he could reach the table leg. By grasping the leg he had pulled himself, on the stretcher, a foot or two across the cabin floor. Now he could touch the German on the shoulder.

"Messner," he was saying. "Messner. I'm talking to you, Messner."

He looked up at the boy.

"He doesn't answer me," he said. "He's been coughing and groaning like hell, and now he doesn't answer." He pulled at the German's jacket. "Messner," he said. "Messner."

The boy bent down by the German, who had turned his face away from the English boy. The blood he had been coughing up had now an amazing and frightening bright- ness on his jacket, the cabin floor and his white face. It was still fresh, and a new stream of it poured out of his mouth with sudden gentleness as the boy moved his head.

With the movement of his head the German let his eyes remain in the direction of the boy. It was clear that he did not see him with his strange and pale unfocussed eyes. "Blood coming out of his mouth," the boy whispered. "All over him. What shall I do?"

"Got your first-aid pack?"

"A box. Yes."

"Let's see what it's got."

While the boy found the first-aid box in Gregson's locker the English boy lay rigid, eyes half closed, as if very tired. The German had begun to moan quietly again now, his head lolling slowly and regularly from side to side, like a mechanical doll, each movement releasing from each corner of his lips a new spit of blood.

The boy opened the first-aid box and laid it by the side of the English pilot, on the floor. But the English boy ignored it, as if he had thought of something else.

"Look under his blanket," he said. "Loosen his clothes a bit. See if you can make him easy. Loosen his jacket and trousers."

The first-aid box lay untouched on the floor. The boy crawled over on his hands and knees to the German, who had never seemed to him quite a human person and now seemed less human, with the doll-like motions of his head, than ever before.

As he drew back the blankets and folded them down to just below the German's waist he saw that a fantastic dark patch had spread itself all across the upper part of his legs and upwards over the left groin. The boy stared at it with the blunted shock of weariness. It was something that did not ask for speculation. The fullness of its violent meaning swept over him for a few slow moments and then engulfed him with the terror of sickness. He felt his teeth crying against each other as he folded the blankets hurriedly back over the body that now and then swayed slightly, helpless and a fraction disturbed, with the motions of the boat and the sea.

He sat on the floor between the two pilots and could not speak for fear of the vast wave of sickness rising up in his throat.

"What is it?" the pilot said.

"Blood," the boy said. "Blood all over him. Legs and stomach."

"Keep him covered," the pilot said.

He spoke with brief finality, checked by his own weariness. He still had his hands on the binoculars, holding them tightly to his chest. He grinned at the boy with flickering, unexpected life.

"Bit bumpy."

"Freshening a bit," the boy said.

"Rain by midday they said. Just time for one patrol. Quite a patrol too."

"Like some tea?" the boy said, and moved as if to get up, but the pilot grinned quietly again and said, "No. No more thanks. Sit and talk to me."

The boy did not know what to say. It seemed to him it would be better if the pilot talked. He had so much more to tell. As a man flying fighters, he had in the eyes of the boy a kind of divinity. Ever since he had first come aboard, with his absurd moustache plastered down on his face, he had seemed not quite real. He had not seemed like other men. He had brought to the boat a casual and magnificent gallantry. The boy longed for him to speak of flying, of aircraft, of speeds: of battles especially. How did it feel up there? He supposed he must often have watched him come over the dunes and the marshes, going out to sea: this same man, and yet not thinking of him as a man but only as something flying, terrific and untouchable, across the sky. He still could not grasp that that furious splendour had a reality now.

All the pilot said was: "It's getting hellish dark in here. Think so?"

"No," the boy said. "It's all right. It's not dark."

"Best of having white hair," the pilot said, and grinned in a very tired, old way at this joke of his.

"I could light the lamp," the boy said.

"Lamp?"

The pilot said the word slowly; he seemed to want to keep it on his lips, for comfort. He looked vaguely upward, desperately trying to see the boy in the small dark cabin. The boy got up. A pair of oil lamps were fastened into the bulkhead between the side lockers, and he now struck a match, to light the one nearer the pilot, on the starboard side. The wind blowing down the companionway through the open door blew out the match, and at the same time the boat lurched and then pitched, so that when he tried to light the second match it wavered in his fingers and went out too. After this he went over and shut the cabin door, and for the first time, with the little light of the doorway shut out, the cabin seemed dark to him also. It seemed dark and small and overcrowded as he stepped back across the bodies of the two men to try to light the lamp for the third time.

And this time he succeeded. The dull orange flame hardly had any light at first. He turned it up. And then when he moved away from it his own shadow fell vast and sombre across the body of the pilot, throwing into tawny edges of relief the yellow varnished panelling and the yellow face of the German beyond.

That shadow in some way discomforted him, and he crouched down. The face of the English boy came full into the oily glow; calm now, moulded by the downward cast of light into a smoother, flatter shape of almost shadowless bone. The boy saw on it as he crouched down the first glimpse of death. It was so unagonized and silent that for a moment or two he almost believed in it. The eyes of the pilot were closed and his lips slightly open, as if the word lamp still remained only partly spoken from them.

Out of this deathly attitude the pilot suddenly opened a pair of eyes that seemed blackened and not awakened by the light of the lamp. They were distorted by a dark and sickly brilliance and the boy was startled. "Better," he heard the pilot say. "Better."

The boy sat hugging his knees with relief.

"How's old Messner?"

"Quiet," the boy said.

"Messner," the pilot said. "How's things? How are you?"

Messner did not answer. He was not groaning now. He had turned his face away from the light of the lamp.

"Hell of a brave sod," the pilot said.

"Might not be him," the boy said. He was not handing out free bravery to any enemy yet.

"I think so," the pilot said. "He knows it was me too."

"You think so?"

"Certain."

"But you were faster, wasn't you?" the boy said. "You could catch him easy, couldn't you? The English are faster, aren't they?"

At last, in a rush, he had spoken his feelings.

"Being fast isn't everything," the pilot said.

"No?"

"Anyway, I wouldn't be as fast. He had a 109. It was just luck."

He grinned, tired, his eyes deadened again.

"Smooth do, though, all the same."

A great quiver of pain suddenly came upward from his body as he finished these words, shaking his whole face with a great vibration of agony, and his eyes lightened bitterly with an awful flash of terror. They did a sudden vivid swirl in the lamplight, like the eyes of someone falling suddenly into space and looking in final horror at something to cling to.

"Snowy," he said. "Snowy," and instinctively the boy caught hold of his hands. They were frantically fixed to the binoculars, glued by awful sweat, and yet cold, and the boy could feel the transmission of pain and coldness flowing out of them into his own.

"God!" the pilot said. "God, good God, good God!"

The agony turned his finger-tips to tangles of frenzied wire, which locked themselves about the boy's hands and could not release them. *The Breadwinner* lurched again, and the boy went hard down on one elbow, unable to save himself and still, even in falling, unable to release himself from the frantic wires of the pilot's hands.

When he managed to kneel upright again he was in a panic at the English boy's sudden silence. It was as if they had both been struggling for possession of the binoculars, and the pilot, tiring suddenly, had lost them.

"I'll get the skipper," the boy said. "I'll fetch Mr. Gregson."

He tried to get up on his feet, but discovered his hands still locked in the pilot's own.

"All right, Snowy. Don't go. All right now. Don't go."

"Sure?" the boy said. "I'd better."

"No. Don't go. Don't. How's old Messner? Have a look at old Messner."

Messner was quiet. The boy, still held by the pilot's hands, could not move. He told the pilot how Messner was quiet, and again that he ought to call Mr. Gregson. The pilot did not answer. The boy had long since lost count of time, and now the half darkness, the lamplight and the silence gave the impression that the day was nearly over.

He crouched there for a long time, imprisoned by the pilot's hands, waiting for him to speak again. He sometimes thought of the binoculars as he sat there. The strap of them and the two sets of fingers seemed inextricably locked together; he felt they would never come apart. And all he could hear was the sound of the pilot's breath, drawn with irregular congested harshness, like the pained echo of rain and sea washing against the timbers of the small ship out-side. He shut his own eyes once, and let himself be swung deeply to and fro by the motions of the ship. He could almost guess by these motions how far they were from shore. At a point about five miles out they struck the current from the river-mouth, faintly at first, but heavier close to land, and on days of westward wind, like this, there was always a cross swell and a pull that would take them up the coast. They still had some way to go.

"Messner all right?"

The voice of the English boy, coming at last, was only a whisper. It seemed to the boy fantastic that there should be this constant question about Messner. He could not conjure any concern for Messner at all, beyond the concern for the binoculars, and he did not speak.

"Valuable bloke, Messner," the pilot said. "Might talk. If we get back."

He tried to grin but the movement of his lips was strengthless, quivering and not very amusing.

"If we get back. That's the big laugh," he said. "Always is." He spoke very slowly now. "When you get back." He tried again with the same dark ineffectiveness to smile. "If you get back."

These ironies were beyond the boy. They served only to accentuate the silence with which the pilot lay looking at him, lips partly open, the continuity of his thought broken down.

And when he spoke again it was of quite different things.

"The lamp's very bright," he said.

"I'll turn it down," the boy said.

"No." His voice had the distance of a whisper gently released in a great hollow. "Rather like it. Lean over a bit."

The shadow of the boy moved across and remained large and protective over the face of the young man. They still gripped each other's fingers tightly, the binocular case between. It seemed very cold, and there was no sound from Messner. The lamp had now and then violent and bright-edged convulsions caused by the plunging of the ship, and the shadow swayed.

It seemed to the boy late in the afternoon when the pilot began to mutter and babble of things he did not understand. Once he opened his eyes with a bright blaze of fantastic vigour, and talked of a girl. The next moment he was saying, "Tell old

Messner he put up a good show. Tell him he's a bastard."

He did not speak again. The boy watched him dying in the vastness of his own shadow without knowing he was dying. It was only when he moved to get a better look at his face that he saw it without even the convulsion of breath. The sound of breathing had stopped, and the moustache, still wet and flat on the face, had now more than ever the look of something mockingly plastered there. The lamp seemed astonishingly bright in its odd distortion, terrifyingly bright in the young immobile eyes that still seemed to be staring straight at the boy.

After some moments he succeeded in getting his fingers out of the dead fingers, at the same time releasing the binoculars. He was cold and he moved quietly, crawling on the cabin floor. When he went over to Messner he found that Messner had died too, and now the lamplight was full on both of them, with equal brightness, as they lay side by side.

THE *BREADWINNER* CAME IN UNDER THE SHELTER OF rain-brown dunes and the western peninsula of the bay in the late afternoon and drove in towards the estuary, with the boy and Gregson on deck. Rain trembling across the darkening sky in grey cascades like spray hid all the further cliffs from sight, and in the distance the hills were lost in cloud. The boy grasped the binoculars in his hands, pressing them against his stomach rather as Gregson pressed the wheel against his own, in the attitude of a man who is about to raise them to his eyes and see what the distances reveal.

"Just turned," Gregson said. "Bleedin' good job for us too. That tide'll come in as high as a church steeple with this wind."

As she came in full across the wind, lumping on the waves as if they had been crests of solid steel, *The Breadwinner* had more than ever the look of a discarded and battered toy. She bumped in a series of jolting short dives that were like the ridiculous mockery of a dance. Her deck as it ran with spray and rain gleamed like dirty yellow ice, so that sometimes when she heeled over and the boy was caught unawares he hung on to the deck-house with one hand, his feet skating outwards. With the other hand he held on to the binoculars. He gripped them with the aggressive tightness of a man who has won a conquest. Nothing, if he could help it, was going to happen to them now.

At times he looked up at the face of Gregson. It was thrust outward into the rain with its own enormous and profound aggression. The boy sometimes could not tell from its muteness whether it was angry or simply shocked into the silences it held for half an hour or more. He wanted to talk to it. There rose up constantly in his mind, tired now and dazed by shock, images of the cabin below. They troubled him more each time he thought of them. Their physical reality began to haunt him much more than the reality of the dead engineer, who lay not ten feet before him, like a piece of sodden and battered merchandise, his blood washed away now by constant rain. He thought often of the conversation of the dead pilot. He thought less often of Messner. There were to him very subtle differences between the men, and death had not destroyed them. When he thought of Messner it was with dry anger. He conceived Messner as the cause of it all. It was something of a low trick. Then he remembered Messner as the man who also carried the binoculars, and he remembered that the binoculars were the only things that had come out of the day that were not sick with the ghastliness of foul and indelible dreams.

He was very tired. The way the sea hit *The Breadwinner* also hit him in the stomach, a dozen times or more a minute, kicking him sore. He had not eaten anything since coming up from the cabin. There had been no more shouts from Gregson, no more cups of tea. Gregson remained for the most part vastly mute, the light beaten out of his face.

When the boy had to talk to him again, he said:

"When will we be in, Mr. Gregson, skipper?"

Gregson did not answer. He kept his face thrust forward into a gigantic pout, angered into a new and tragic sullenness. The boy had not known this face before. There were times when he had been afraid of Gregson; they were separated by what seemed to him vast stretches of years by the terrifying vastness of the man. Now he was comforted by the gigantic adultness of Gregson. It shut him away, for a time, from the things he had seen.

They were coming in towards the estuary now, Gregson giving the wheel a hard point or two to port, and then another, and then holding *The Breadwinner* hard down, her head a point or two west from north. The face of the sea was cresting down a fraction; the wind gave a suck or two at the sail as the boat turned and lay over, loosing it back as she straightened. The boy could see the shore clearly now, misty with rain, the dunes in long wet brown stripes, the only colour against the winter land beyond. And suddenly, looking up at Gregson, he thought for a moment he detected there a slight relaxation on the enormous bulging face. He saw Gregson lick the rain from his tired lips. It gave him courage to think that at last Gregson was going to speak again.

"Almost in, Mr. Gregson, skipper," he said.

The violence of Gregson's voice was so sudden that it was like the clamour of a man frightened by his own anger.

"God damn them!" he roared. "God damn them! All of them, God damn them! Why don't they let us alone? Why don't they let us alone! Why don't they let us alone! How much longer? Why don't they let our lives alone? God damn and blast them—all of them, all of them, all the bastards, all over the world!"

Gregson finished shouting and gave an enormous fluttering sigh. It seemed to exhaust him. He stood heavy and brooding across the wheel, his body without savagery, his face all at once dead and old and colourless, the rain streaming down it like a flood of tears.

He put his hand on the boy's shoulder, as if he now suddenly remembered he was there. The sea was calming down at the mouth of the estuary, and *The Breadwinner* was beginning to run lumpily in towards the narrow gap in the steel defences, rusty for miles along the wild and empty shore. There were no lights in the dark afternoon, and the rain darkened a little more each moment the farther hills, the cliffs and the low sky. The boy did not move again. All the time he had wanted, at this last moment, to raise the binoculars to his eyes. For some reason he did not want to raise them now. There did not seem much use in raising them. He was not even sure that there seemed much use in possessing them. As he stood there with Gregson's arm on his shoulder he remembered the dead engineer; he remem- bered Gregson's violent outburst of words; and he remembered the dead pilots, lying in the orange lamplight in the small cabin darkened by his own shadow with their dead fair faces, side by side. And they became for him, at that moment, all the pilots, all the dead pilots, all over the world.

At that moment they ran into the mouth of the estuary. Gregson continued tenderly to hold him by the shoulder, not speaking, and the boy once more looked up at him, seeing the old tired face again as if bathed in tears. He did not speak, and there rose up in him a grave exultation.

He had been out with men to War and had seen the dead. He was alive and *The Breadwinner* had come home.